This book is dedicated to all of the
children living through the 2020
COVID-19 pandemic.

Hi! My name is Sofie. I live in New York City and this is me, celebrating my birthday this year. You may ask, "Why are you wearing a mask?" or, "Why are you celebrating outside with balloons on a car?" I am here to explain.

The last week at school was just like all of the others. It was filled with fun activities and normal routines.

On Sunday, my family and I went to the beach. We played in the sand, but my parents said we couldn't play in the playground. They made sure we washed our hands really well when we got home. It seemed like things were a little different than usual.

That evening my mom and dad told me that schools would be
closing because of a virus.
"Coronavirus or COVID-19," is what they called it on television.

I had a lot of questions. I remembered having viruses
before, but schools had never closed. Why were they
closing now?

They explained that this virus, COVID-19, is different. It is very contagious.
That means it passes from one person to another very easily.

It has also made a lot of people very sick. I was starting to feel worried.
My parents reassured me, "This is not forever."

That Monday, we began doing things very differently. We had new routines. We didn't go to school. Instead, my teachers sent activities on the computer and I did them at home with my mom. My little brother and sister joined in, too. We sent pictures of our work to my teacher. My dad said this is called remote learning.

Mom is having us do lots of inside activities. Creating art masterpieces, exploring science experiments, and cooking healthy foods are some of my favorites.

We started doing some special family activities in the house, too. We love having movie nights, fort building, and playing hide and seek... in the dark!

I am having lots of fun at home, but I am definitely missing my teachers and friends from school. Luckily, I get to see them during our live meetings and through video lessons.

Sometimes the videos from my teachers make me feel sad. I miss seeing them everyday. I miss playing with my friends. I see that my parents are upset too. They try to be strong, but sometimes when they are watching the news, I see them cry, because even grown ups cry. But then they remind me, *this is not forever.*

Before COVID-19, we used to go out to dinner. I loved to act fancy at restaurants, but now restaurants and lots of stores are closed to help stop the spread of the virus. So, I made my own restaurant at home called "Sofie's Café." I am the chef and my brother is the waiter!

It's lots of fun, but I can't wait to go to a real restaurant again.

Although lots of places are closed, there are people called essential workers who still report to work each day.

These people keep our community going and are very brave.

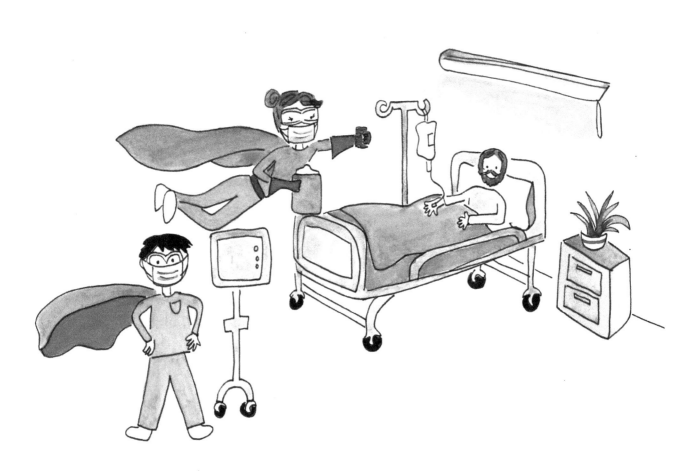

Maybe the bravest of all are the healthcare workers. Those are the doctors, nurses, and hospital workers helping all of the people who are sick with the virus to get better. They are like real life super heroes.

Each night at 7 o'clock, my family and I go out on our terrace to clap for those super heroes. We play music really loudly, and all of our neighbors come out to clap and cheer too.

This makes us all feel hopeful. That means, feeling good about the future. We can be hopeful because we know that *this is not forever*.

In order to stay safe, we all need to stay home. When we go out for walks, we should stay six feet apart from others. There are signs posted to show us that distance. We also wear a mask or face covering to keep germs from spreading. All of these actions are part of what is called social distancing.

When we come back inside, it is very important to wash our hands REALLY well. We sing the happy birthday song two times to make sure our hands are really clean... Hey, that brings me back to my birthday!

Today is my birthday. I couldn't have the party that we had planned. My friends, family, and I need to stay safe by staying apart. Instead of a party, we are having a birthday parade! They are all driving by my house right now. They have balloons and signs and they are honking their horns like crazy! I want to give them all hugs and kisses, but for today this is awesome. I know we will all be together again soon.

This is not forever.

Author and illustrator, Kristen Meehan, is a New York City public school teacher. She is also the mother of three young children (Sofie, 5, Lucas, 3, and Charlotte, 1). This story is based on their experience in Brooklyn, New York, during this historic pandemic. Every night, after kissing her children and putting them to bed, working on this project gave her hope. Her wish is that this book helps children to cope during this confusing time. She wants to thank her family for all of their support throughout the creation of this project. A special thanks goes out to her husband, Rob, who reports to work everyday as an essential NYC worker. This is her first book.

CPSIA information can be obtained
at www.ICGtesting.com
Printed in the USA
BVHW022240140820
586439BV00002B/75